Qu'Appelle

By DAVID BOUCHARD ⊕ *Paintings by* MICHAEL LONECHILD

RAINCOAST BOOKS

Vancouver

If you walk out on the prairie
When the sun is westward fading
When a gentle breeze is blowing
And you think that you're alone,

If you walk out on the prairie
When the sun is westward fading
If by chance you hear a calling
If you think you hear a calling …

Listen carefully, do not answer
Do not stir and do not answer
Listen carefully, you might come to hear
A voice call, "Qui Appelle?"

Cree Village

There are many who have heard this voice

Lamenting in the evening breeze

Many here have heard this voice

That calls out, "Qui Appelle?"

The story that the Elders tell

Is of a brave who lost his love

The Elders tell an ancient tale

A tale of deep and sacred love.

Walk out on the prairie

When the sun is westward fading

Listen carefully, you might come to hear

A voice call, "Qui Appelle?"

Returning Hunters

Spring Time

They say that two small children
Fell in love before they learned to walk.
They say they learned to think as one
Before they learned to walk or talk.

They tell of how these children
Learned by listening to their Elders
Learned the customs of their people
Learned their customs and traditions.

They tell of how these children
Were together day and night
That there never had been closer friends
Two beings who shared one heart.

It was custom when death called upon
A brave who left a family
That neighbours who knew this man
Would make his child their own.

Thus when Ikciv lost his father
He was lodged with sweet Witonia
It seemed natural that the two young friends
Share both their homes and hearts.

The New Beginning

The Young Warriors

The children grew and prospered
Learned to care for one another
Learned to care and share together
Learned to lead with mind and heart
Learned to play and work together
Every day, they grew together
It is said their love was such
That they could never be apart.

A friendship like a legend grew
Across the plain, all nations knew
There never had been two like these
The pride of every Cree.

A girl who had the strength and heart
Of any two young fighting braves
A girl who rode and fought and danced
As well as any strong young brave.

And Ikciv, too, for all to see
Did lead his kin through more than words
The spirit of his Elders shone
Through his each and every deed.

Dear Reader — you must never doubt

The strength of love's swift arrow

As one morning these two rose to find

Their friendship had matured into

The kind of passion that is found

In one in every million.

They were betrothed through sacred love

That made their lives a legend.

Falling in Love

The Sun Dance

Yet sadly not all things are just,
Some customs just cannot be changed.
The brave young maiden could but watch
The Sun Dance from the trees.

She felt the pain as her love was pierced
The bone cut deep into his flesh
They say she somehow bore the scars
(Love's power can be strange).

She glowed with pride, yet even then
She worried knowing that one day
He'd have to leave her on her own
She'd never spent one day alone …

The day they feared did finally come
When all young men were called to war.
No woman could, no woman should,
Their paths had both been clearly laid.

They cried and swore to Manito
They'd find some way to make it through,
No matter how or when or where
They'd somehow find a way.

Through tears he left her by the lake
And rode his pony westward.
This raid would take two weeks or less,
He led the party westward.

Going After the Horse Thieves

The Medicine Man

Can you explain a baby's birth
To those who have stopped trying?
What power sends the reaper's glove
To take the life of youth in love?

How illness comes at times like these
Is one of life's strange mysteries.
The brave was barely out of sight
When his love fell ill, that very night.

They treated her with oils and herbs,
She should have soon recovered.
The old ones could her fever tend
But not her heart, it would not mend.

The Elders tell of how a brave

Fought driven like a beast possessed

He fought with passion, won much praise

And victory with each crushing blow.

But he'd not stay and dance that night

He'd return to his love Witonia

Not knowing that she'd fallen ill

Not knowing that she'd taken ill.

No, he'd not stay for one more night

He'd rush home to his love Witonia

He lived to be there, by the side

Of his love, his life, Witonia.

Caught Up With the Horse Thieves

I Hear a Voice

He lay to rest along a lake
Fatigued from days of fighting.
He lay down to sleep along a lake
When he heard a distant calling …

"Who's calling?" he cried … "I know your voice
I'm here, my love, I'm coming."
He rode his mount back into the night
To answer his loved one's calling …

He was covered with sweat and his eyes were wet
When again he heard the calling.
"Qui Appelle?" he cried. Yet he knew deep inside
It was she, his love, who was calling.

His soul felt the cold as he rode into camp
To his village distressed and in mourning.
He dropped to his knees by an Elder and asked,
"Was it she? Was it she I heard calling?"

The Elder looked up to the sky far above,
With a gentle but distant voice answered,
"She called out your name, first once then again
Cried, 'I've tried but I can't live without you.'"

The Passing

Setting Sun

He laid his head upon his love
Where he sobbed for days like a baby.
Then he finally called out to the maker above,
Called through sadness and tears and through anger.

"You would never have taken her far from my side!
You would never have done such a cruel, horrid thing!"
Then he rose without talking, turned back to the lake —
The creator could not have done such a cruel thing.

He walked to their tent, took a few of her things
With his head down, strode right by his people
And he pushed his canoe hard onto the lake
Where he set off in search of the love of his life
Where he set off in search of Witonia.

If you walk out on the prairie

When the sun is westward fading

When a gentle breeze is blowing

And you think that you're alone,

Listen carefully, do not answer

Do not stir and do not answer

Listen carefully, you might come to hear

A voice call, "Qui Appelle?"

Lone Wolf Warrior

The Valley, the People and the Legend
A note from the poet ...

I write this at home, on my prairie, as I travel across the beautiful Qu'Appelle Valley.

After being away for twelve years, I am finally home — thinking about the legend that most prairie children hear at some time in their lives. There are different versions of the story and I write it as it was told to me.

The Qu'Appelle Valley follows the Qu'Appelle River for more than 400 kilometres, from Manitoba into the heartland of Saskatchewan. It is a welcome escape from the endless plain around it. The valley is green and lush, alive with birds, beasts and running water. It boasts four spectacular lakes, often known as The Calling Lakes: Katepwa, Mission, Pasqua and Echo. The name Katepwa comes from the Cree word *kab-tep-was*. It means "river that calls."

For centuries the Cree people, who still own and inhabit much of this land, found shelter from our cruel winters in the Qu'Appelle Valley. Here they found fuel and food. Wildlife gathered in the hills and coulees, and the lakes offered a healthy diet of fish.

It wasn't until the late 1700s that voyageurs and missionaries first appeared on the scene. It was one of these newcomers, a Métis trader named Daniel Harmon, who first reported that the Cree people throughout the valley spoke of a voice that cried out to them. Their response was "Who calls?" — in French, "Qui Appelle?"

This legend has been passed from generation to generation by word of mouth. The only written account I know is by the Mohawk poet Pauline Johnson. Her telling is significantly different from the version I was told, and the way in which Michael and I share it with you.

Edited by Scott Steedman
Designed by Ingrid Paulson

Raincoast Books   In the United States:
9050 Shaughnessy Street   Publishers Group West
Vancouver, British Columbia   1700 Fourth Street
Canada   Berkeley, California
V6P 6E5   94710
www.raincoast.com

Raincoast Books acknowledges the ongoing financial support of the Government of Canada through The Canada Council for the Arts and the Book Publishing Industry Development Program (BPIDP); and the Government of British Columbia through the BC Arts Council.

National Library of Canada Cataloguing in Publication Data

Bouchard, Dave, 1952–
    Qu'appelle

    ISBN 1-55192-475-7

    1. Cree Indians—Folklore. 2. Legends—Saskatchewan. I. Lonechild, Michael. II. Title.
E99.C88B68 2002   j398.2'097124'02   C2001-911680-2

Library of Congress Control Number: 2002102454

Printed and bound in Hong Kong

1 2 3 4 5 6 7 8 9 10

ACKNOWLEDGEMENTS
"I could never have hoped to write such a poem without feeling that very love deep within me. This is for you dear wife. This is for you Vicki."
D.B.

"Thanks to my wife Sarah and my stepdaughter Keagan for posing for me. And to Jack and Rita Klassen of The Bronze Rooster Gallery, for their involvement in the process."
M.L.